Dodi's Prince

ILLUSTRATED BY

Jacqueline Rogers

DUTTON CHILDREN'S BOOKS / NEW YORK

Dodi's Prince

Vaughn Michaels

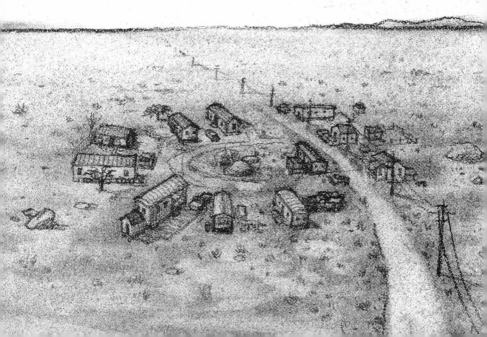

Library of Congress Cataloging-in-Publication Data

Michaels, Vaughn.
Dodi's Prince / by Vaughn Michaels;
illustrated by Jacqueline Rogers.—1st ed.
p. cm.
Summary: Eight-year-old Dodi hopes to overcome the objections
of her family and Texas trailer park neighbors so that she can keep
the stray dog she calls Prince.
ISBN: 0-525-47034-4
[1. Dogs—Fiction. 2. Pets—Fiction. 3. Trailer camps—Fiction.
4. Texas—Fiction.]
I. Rogers, Jacqueline, ill. II. Title.
PZ7.M58134 Do 2003
[Fic]—dc21   2002074149

Published in the United States 2003 by Dutton Children's Books,
a division of Penguin Putnam Books for Young Readers
345 Hudson Street, New York, New York 10014
www.penguinputnam.com

Designed by Tim Hall
Printed in USA
First Edition
1 3 5 7 9 10 8 6 4 2

Dodi's Prince

CHAPTER

1

*N*ame's Dodi Tanner. I live here in the desert, way out in Texas. Or as Momma would say, way out in the middle of nowhere. Except it's not nowhere exactly. We got us a store with a post-office window, and a Texaco, where Daddy works, and the Desert Rose—that's the café. And the trailer park where we live along with other folks. We even have a school, in a double-wide. But not the high schoolers. They don't have a school. They have to travel down the blacktop an hour to Fort Bennett. An hour there, an hour back. Every school day. Plus we got a name— it's not Nowhere, it's Apache Springs. 'Cept I never seen hide nor hair of no Apache, and the spring dried up years back.

Dodi's not my real name. Real name's Dorothea Kathleen Tanner. Momma named me after her momma. But Daddy said I was just a bitty thing when I was born. Said I looked more like a little Dodi noodle than some highfalutin Dorothea Kathleen. So I became Dodi. No complaints here. One thing I ain't, it's highfalutin. Whatever that means.

Actually, I *did* have me a complaint. It was this: ever since Josie moved away, I didn't have me a friend to play with. Josie and her mom pulled up stakes one night. I woke up, looked out the window, and their trailer was plumb gone. No *adiós, amigo* or anything. Only thing left in their spot was trash and weeds and tire tracks. How do you like that? Jesse—he's my brother—he had Dickey Martin, but I didn't have anyone. Well, there were the twins, but they were too young to be much fun. The twins are my brothers too. That makes three brothers and no sisters. Not even one. And it was summer. Things were getting mighty lonely, let me tell you.

Then one day, all that changed. That was the day I got me a friend. A best friend. The bestest friend anyone could ask for.

Actually, getting him was the easy part. It was hanging on to him that was work. Pure work.

2

*T*his here is how I met him, my soon-to-be very best friend.

It was morning. I had just finished helping Momma with the breakfast dishes when she said, "Go." I grabbed my quilt. It's just a wore-out baby blanket, but it makes a good pretend cape. I hopped down the steps and slammed the door shut.

"Don't slam that door," Momma yelled. Uh-oh— forgot. I waited. When I didn't hear anything more, I hopped over to the rusty tank, catty-whompus to our trailer.

I leaned against the tank. *"Eeow!"* It was some kind of hot. Hot, like sizzling bacon. And no won-

6

der; this being July, it had been frying in the sun that morning. In the desert old man sun can cook metal quick. I gave my finger a lick. I poked the tank again. "Sssssssss," I hissed as my finger heated up.

I went over to our hose, took ahold of the nozzle, and gave the spigot a twist. Water spurted out—first hot, then cool. I wrestled the hose—a snarled rubber snake—and watered that tank down. Gave it a good bath. Squirted myself too. I poked the tank again—bearable now.

Down went the hose. There is a cinder block to one side of the tank that I use to climb aboard. The tank is too old to hold propane like before, so I get to play on it. It makes a dandy pretend horse: an Arabian stallion, pure white with a silky mane. Name of Prince.

"Stay, Prince," I said. My Prince minds pretty good. Not all the time but most times. I reached around for the quilt and slung it over my shoulders so it fanned out over the back of the tank, prettylike.

"Stay, Prince." Prince was starting to act up. "Easy," I said.

"Good boy." I patted his neck, grabbed a handful of pretend mane.

"Walk, Prince," I said. I closed my eyes.

I gave Prince two taps with my heels—not too hard—to make him speed up. I started to bounce up and down, up and down, as Prince broke into a trot. You can't trot too long: too hard on the seat. I gave Prince another kick, a little harder, and said, "Giddyup," and *tarump, tarump, tarump,* away we went. Soon we were loping along, watching the scenery go by. Not for real, of course. This was still pretend.

When Prince gallops, it's real smooth. Up and down, up and down, like in a boat. Like when the waves raise you up and set you down, soft and gentle. Leastways, I think it's like a boat. I never been in a boat.

So I was on Prince's back, watching the scenery go by on my eyelids—on account of my eyes being closed—and I noticed the rocks and tumbleweeds getting teensier and teensier. Why? 'Cause we were flying through air. Prince can do that. He was moving his feet, pawing the air like a swimmer through water. A powerful swimmer. Higher and higher we went, skimming the clouds. I could see all the trailers in Apache Springs. They were scattered below

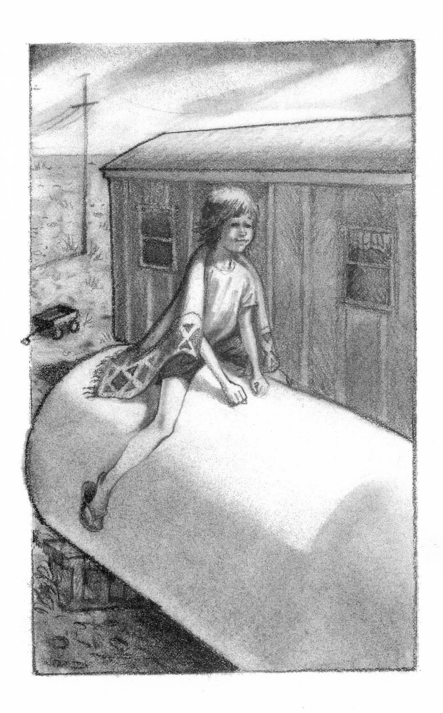

like pencil boxes. There was the blacktop. Sitting beside it was the Desert Rose, and Ragland's Grocery with the post-office window, and the Texaco. And over yonder, snuggling like a pair of plumb horny toads, was two brown baldy mountains, Little Toad and Big Toad. Running down the face of Big Toad was a long pale line, standing out like a scar against the nut brown mountain. That was Satan's slide. I've never climbed up that far. Jesse has. Him and Dickey. Then they slid down Satan's slide. Jesse wore a hole in his britches. He said it was the most fun he'd ever had. I asked him was he scared, and he said "Naw." But he was, I could tell. Someday, I'm going to climb up there and slide all the way down that mountain, just like Jesse, scared or no.

Me and Prince circled back for another look-see. We flew over the Bulldog's trailer. Her name's Mizz Bullock, but I call her the Bulldog 'cause she's got these hangie-down jowls and is mean as a bulldog. Meaner even. I can spot her trailer because she has a patio. Hers is the only trailer with one. Most people don't stick around long enough to put down anything permanent. 'Cept us, of course. We been here for as long as I can remember. But Momma won't let Daddy put one in. I don't think Momma wants us to be permanent either.

Me and Prince sailed over Mrs. Robinson's place. She's nice. She has a real house—she's permanent too. Her house is made out of cinder blocks that Mr. Robinson painted green. Momma likes it. The green color reminds her of where she lived when she was a little girl. Even Mrs. Robinson's house was tiny up here. There was Mrs. Robinson working in her yard, no bigger than a doodlebug.

"Hallooo, Mrs. Robinson," I started to yell. Up went my hand to wave when—holy cow—I started teetering over.

"Whoa! Whoa, Prince!" I yelled. But Prince didn't whoa. What the heck? He can be stubborn, but Prince has never not stopped. Not till now. Next thing I knew I was tumbling off his back. Backwards. Over I went, cape and all. It was scary. I reckoned I was fixing to break every bone in my body. Then *whomp*.

I opened one eye. Then t'other. I was flat on my stomach, in the mud—'cause I forgot to turn off the water—and nose-to-sticker to a sticker bush.

I lay there, trying to catch my breath. My cape was covering me like a patchwork tent. I felt a tug. Then another. Jerk, it went. Jerk, jerk. It's Jesse, I was thinking, what jerked me off the tank. He must of grabbed hold of my cape and pulled me off. Backwards. Jesse's ten. I'm eight. He's bigger than me, but that don't mean he gets the better of me. Nosirree.

Jerk, jerk. There he went again. What did he think he was doing? Didn't he realize I could have broken every bone in my body? I twisted around to tell him off. "Jesse, you, you poophead you," I sputtered. "You are going to be one sorry . . ."

Hello? What was this?

It wudn't Jesse. Nosirree. Not even close.

CHAPTER

3

*W*hy lookie there—it was a dog.

He was a little scudder, all black, every bit black except a pinch of white chin whiskers. He had him a grip on my quilt, and he was pulling and tugging for all he was worth, all the while watching me out of two of the blackest marbly eyes you ever saw.

"Hey, little doggie," I said. I moved my hand to him, slow, for him to sniff. Only he didn't sniff. He kept pulling and tugging.

I reached to pet him. He let go of the quilt and hopped away. "Hey, little fella. Don't be scared," I said low, so's not to frighten him. "I won't hurt you."

I wiggled closer on my knees. I reached out once

more. He let me brush his nose but again hopped away, only not as far this time. I eased closer still. Ever so softly my fingers skimmed his nose. Then slowly I trailed them across his cheek, through the fur on his neck, down his side. He was leaning away. He had a bead on me with those black marbly eyes, but he stood his ground. Soon I was petting him up.

"Nice dog," I said. "Pretty dog." Actually, he wudn't all that pretty. He had tangles and mud daubs around his paws.

I was up close now, using both hands, rubbing deep into his fur. "That feels good, don't it, boy?"

I could tell he liked it, so I answered for him. "Yup," I said. His eyes lazed down.

Just then, *bam*, the trailer door sprang open. Out clumped Jesse. "Hey," he said. "Where'd that dog come from?"

The little dog scooted away. He ran into the road, stopped, and looked back. That there is a dirt road that runs in front of our trailer.

"Now see what you did," I wailed at Jesse. "You scared him off."

"Where'd he come from?" asked Jesse.

"Don't know," I said. "Never seen him before."

Jesse bent down. He patted his leg and let out a low whistle. "Here, boy," he said. "Come here. Come on."

But Prince—that was what I had decided to call him. I guess you can tell that's one of my favorite names. Anyway, Prince didn't move. He stuck his nose up and tested the air. Jesse straightened and started toward him. Prince let out a yip and scooted farther away. Now he was clean on t'other side of the road by Pop Riddle's cactus garden.

"Aww," Jesse said. He slapped the air and turned to leave. "He's just a stupid mutt."

"He is not," I yelled at Jesse's back. "He's Prince." But Jesse didn't hear me, or he pretended he didn't. Either way he was gone, out of the yard, over to Dickey Martin's to play. Good riddance—he didn't know a good dog from a cow pie.

I turned my attention back to Prince. He was taking everything in like he understood what was being said—like he knew it was him being talked about. I started across the road, taking baby steps so's not to spook him again. He sat calmlike, watching me come closer.

Soon I was petting him up again, wiggling my

fingers deep into his fur to scratch his skin—he liked that—when Momma stuck her head out the trailer and yelled, "Dodi?"

"Yes, Momma?" I yelled back.

"Come here," she said.

Oh, phooey. "Bye, bye," I said to Prince, and started back across the road. I turned to look at him. "Don't you go away now. I'll be back."

CHAPTER

4

When I got to the steps, Momma opened the door and handed out Mickey. I put him on the bottom step between my legs because I knew what was coming next. Yup. Momma reached around and passed me Mac. Mickey and Mac are the twins. They're one and a half apiece.

She told me, "Dodi, watch the twins while I do the laundry."

"Yes ma'am," I said. Those twins, they were just learning to walk, and they were a handful—both hands. A couple of strong legs didn't hurt neither. Mine, not theirs.

Then Momma came down the steps with a load of clothes. I hauled Mac out of the way. "Make sure you keep your eye on them," Momma said as she headed to the washateria. That's the shed that has a washing machine for the trailer folks to use. I reached down for Mickey and—howdy!—he was gone. I spun around and there he was, teetering through the yard, swinging his bottle by the nipple.

"Stay," I commanded Mac, twin number two. I took out after twin number one.

I corralled Mickey by the arm. He commenced to twist and whine. He was about to erupt, so I stooped down and said, "Wagon? Want to go for a ride in the wagon, Mickey?" His face brightened, bunching into a sloppy grin.

Mickey and Mac love their Radio Flyer. Was I glad when Daddy brought it home. I plop them in, and they're happy as pigs at chow time. And speaking of pigs, they are a couple of oinkers, and that wagon saves on toting them around. Or chasing after them.

So that was where we were—they were in their wagon, and I was pulling them along the road. I pulled them near Prince, who was laying in the shade by Pop Riddle's bus. Pop lives in an old yellow school bus with the seats taken out.

Prince was watching us with those black eyes, his tongue lolling out. I stopped before I got too close. The wagon might have scared him off. The twins were quiet. They were looking at Prince. And Prince was looking at them. They were sizing one another up.

Prince pulled himself to his feet. He made his way over. I reckoned he was thinking, they smell funny, but seem harmless. He poked his nose into Mickey's cheek. Whoa, Mickey went. He pulled back, a look on his face like, where'd that come from. Then Prince reached over and slurped his tongue across Mac's face. Mac slapped his cheeks and let out a squeal, *"Eeeeee."* Then Mickey let out a squeal. Then they leaned forward and grabbed four fists of fur.

"Oh no," I said. They may be small but they're strong, and I was afraid they'd hurt Prince. I shook their hands loose. "Like this," I said. I flattened their hands and showed them how to pet Prince nice.

They started going to town on him, first one hand,

then the other, then both—and none too gentle. But Prince didn't mind. Whenever they slowed, he wiggled against them, causing them to squeal and start up again. Sometimes they'd snatch a handful of doggie hair and pull it toward their mouths. But by the time their fists got that far, the hair had pulled out the other end, and they ended up with a mouthful of fingers.

You could tell Prince was taken with them, though it was hard to see why. Reckon it was because he's a good dog. He was drooping against them, half in their wagon. They were laughing and blubbering "Doggie" over and over.

We all played with Prince for a while. I'd found me a stick to toss. Prince would run and grab it and bring it back. Only he wouldn't come all the way. He would stop out of reach. When I made a grab for it, he'd scoot out of reach again. He'd do this three or four times before he'd let me take ahold. Then he wouldn't let go, and we'd have us a tug-of-war. Finally he'd loosen his grip, and I'd go back to the wagon for another toss. He'd follow behind, keeping a watch on that stick like it was a T-bone steak.

Sometimes I'd just pretend to throw the stick and

jam it in the wagon between the twins. But Prince caught on. He'd put his front paws on the wagon and nose the boys out of the way. That'd make them laugh. They'd grab and pull him this way and that. He'd bark and lick their faces.

Just about then I saw Momma coming back with a clean load of clothes. Prince looked up too. He dropped the stick and ran to her. He wiggled this little dance in front of her feet, almost tripping Momma up.

"Scat," Momma said. "Get away, dog." She took a swipe at Prince with her foot but missed. Prince scatted like he was told. He ran to some weeds and hunkered down.

"Dodi," Momma said over her shoulder, "bring the twins back now. It's time for their lunch." She laid the load under the clothesline. "I need you to hang these," she said. "And mind, Dodi, be careful—this time." She gave me a warning look under pinched eyebrows. That was because last time, I knocked the basket over in the dirt, and Momma had to wash half the load over. Only it wudn't my fault. It was Jesse's. He was teasing me, and when I reached back to give him a swat, which he was asking for, the basket tumbled over. Momma don't like dirt. She fights it all the time. But when you live smack in the middle of a desert, I figger it's a heck of a lot easier to just say howdy and make friends with it. Like me.

I pulled Mickey and Mac to our trailer, tires crunching gravel. Momma hoisted them inside. Before she closed the door, she added, "When you're through with the clothes, come in yourself for a bite to eat."

I started hanging. I got me a couple more cinder blocks that I use to reach the lines. I was going along good, developing a rhythm. I'd reach in the basket for something—a T-shirt or diaper—fold one corner over the line, snag a clothespin out of the bag, and pin it into place. It was reach, fold, pin; reach, fold, pin. I could even do it with my eyes closed, so I did. Reach, fold, pin. Reach, fold, pin. I could smell the Clorox coming off the clothes, feel the sun warming my scalp.

I was on a "reach" when, instead of something damp and soft, I felt something dry and fuzzy. I took a peek. It was Prince sitting in the clothes basket. Just like nobody's business.

"What are you doing? You can't get in there," I said, even though he already was. "Out, Prince." He hopped out. He minded right off, but the damage was done: muddy footprints all over one of Momma's flowered pillowcases.

"Oh no," I said. "Now see what you done?" I took the pillowcase out and held it in front of his face and pointed at the brown smudges. "How am I going to get these out?" Prince didn't offer any suggestions. "And after what Momma said."

Starting to panic, I looked around and noticed the hose. I took the case over, turned on the water, and soaked it. Then I scrubbed at the spots with my fingers. I rubbed my fingertips red trying to get those stains out. They faded to a tinge. I wrung out the case, took it back to the line, and hung it up. When I stepped back, it appeared to me that the brown smudges blended right in with the yellow roses on the case. And anyway, that was as clean as it was going to get.

"Don't you do that again. Naughty dog. Naughty, naughty," I said. I looked around, but Prince wudn't paying me any mind. He was over by the hose trying to lap up water from a mud hole. "Ugh. Don't drink that. That's dirty water." He kept on lapping. So I got down off my block, went and fetched a tin pail the twins use to make dirt castles. I rinsed it out and filled it with fresh water. I put it in front of Prince, and he drank and drank and drank like he hadn't had a drink in a long time.

I finished hanging the wash and went inside for my favorite sandwich: peanut butter and jelly wrapped up in a tortilla. But before I did, I took Prince's head in my hands and said, "I'll be right back out. Just in case you'd like to play some more."

And when I finished eating and came back outside, there he was. So I reckon he did want to play some more, so we did all afternoon. We played fetch the stick, find the stick, tug-of-war with the stick, keep away with the stick. We was having so much fun I didn't notice my shadow getting long until the afternoon was near gone.

The clothes had long since dried. I decided to take them down and fold them without having to be reminded. I was careful to fold the flowered pillowcase so the dirt spots, which you couldn't even see, were on the inside.

"Dodi." That was Momma. She had stuck her head out from around the trailer door and was motioning me to come on. Then she disappeared inside.

"Coming," I said. I turned to Prince. "I have to go in to help with supper now, so I got to say good-bye." He cocked his head to one side, and I scratched behind his ears. "You better go home now." He cocked his head to the other side. "Home. You go home now." But he just sat there looking at me. I looked around to make sure no one was watching, then gave him a kiss on the tip of his nose. It was cold and wet. It tickled too. I got up and started for the trailer. When I turned around, Prince was sitting there—hadn't moved a smidgen—watching me leave.

I helped Momma get the supper on. Daddy came home from work, and we all crowded around our kitchen table. Supper is a production, so by the time the dishes were done, it was bedtime, and I didn't get outside to check on Prince. But I saved two crème-filled sandwich cookies—my dessert—in case he'd be there the next day. After I went to my room, I stood on my bed, cupped my hands around my eyes, and mashed my face up against the window to see if I could spot the little dog. But all I seen was black. I went to sleep under the roar of our swamp cooler, hoping, oh hoping, Prince would be there in the morning.

CHAPTER

5

*N*ext morning I woke to Momma doing dishes—
clink, clatter, splash. That was my signal to get up.
Did you ever notice how loud everything sounds
when you're trying to nab one last wink? Especially
when the sink is just t'other side of a paper-thin
wall. Momma was doing up Daddy's breakfast
dishes. He'd already left for the gas station. I decided to get up and dressed before Momma had to
yell—no sense hitting a sour note first thing.

I bumped my night table and off went two crème-
filled sandwich cookies. What? Oh yeah—Prince,
that cute little doggie. Reckon he's still there?
Probably not. Probably went home by now. But

maybe so. Maybe he don't have a home. Maybe he needs a home. That got me stirring. I decided to run outside and check before another minute'd passed. I took two steps and was in the hall. One good thing coming from being the only girl—my own room. It may be no bigger than a rabbit hutch, but it's *my* rabbit hutch.

I was at the door when Momma said, "Young lady, where do you think you are going in your pajamas?"

I ran back to my room, tossed off my pj's, shrugged into my shirt and shorts, and slipped on my flip-flops. I jammed the cookies into a pocket, just in case.

I was at the door a second time when Momma said, "Dodi, is your bed made?"

"No ma'am," I said, heading back.

I wrestled the bed together, stood back to admire my work—one end of the spread was trailing linoleum, the other showing mattress. I yanked it straight. I punched up the pillow, jamming my pj's underneath.

I was at the door a third time when "Dodi," said Momma, "get the boys up, then sit down for breakfast." Golly, I liked to have never gotten outside at that rate.

The boys were up. I was wolfing down cornflakes. In between spoonfuls I popped up to look out the window to see if I could spy Prince. I couldn't.

"Dodi," Momma said, "what's wrong with you? You got ants in your pants? What's your problem?"

"Hmm," I said, and shrugged my shoulders. "No problem." Which was the truth because Prince wudn't no problem, way I figgered.

But then Jesse piped up, "Bet she's looking for that dog."

"What dog?" Momma wanted to know.

"That mongrel hanging around yesterday. All day. Like it thinks this here is its home," said Jesse.

"How do you know what he thinks, Mr. Smarty?" I said.

"Never mind what it thinks," Momma said. "This isn't its home, and don't go getting some crazy notion about keeping a dog." Then she added, "Just what I need, more work."

I was about to say Prince won't be no work but decided to let it go. Didn't reckon Momma was in any mood to hear an argument out of me. I started to clear the table, but my mind was so fixed on that

dog that a breakfast bowl jumped plumb out of my hand, sloshing soggy flakes. I no more than got that sopped up when I clattered two spoons to the floor. Before I had time to pick them up, Momma spun me around and shoved me toward the door.

"Go," she said. "Go now before you do any more damage."

Outside, at first I didn't see Prince. I looked all around, but no dog. Dang. Dang. Double dang. My shoulders sagged. I felt like someone had stuck me with a pin and let the air out. *U-u-u-ugh*. Like that. I went over to a cinder block and sat myself down.

I reached into my pocket for a cookie. No use letting them go to waste. I twisted one apart. Just as I was about to teeth off the creamy inside, I heard something. Not sure what. I twirled around. It was Prince. He was crawling up behind me, on his belly, Injun style.

"Well, howdy, little fella. I knew you'd be here. I just knew it." Now I felt like that pin was out, the hole patched, and I was filling up with each breath.

Prince stopped when his scraggly paws tipped the block. He looked up between his bushy brows. Not at me. At what was in my hands—the two cookie halves. His eyes rolled from one hand to the other. His eyebrows too. Back and forth they went.

I held my hand down. He surveyed every bit of that cookie, sniffing away. Then he started to lick off the filling. He licked and licked. The filling melted into the cookie, and the cookie melted into my palm. When it was one soggy mess, he pinched it off with his teeth. Then he licked my fingers clean.

The other half he took in one piece. Munched it in two. Half fell in the dirt.

"Uh-oh," I said, and reached down to pick it up. Prince didn't object, but he didn't take his eyes off me. Not for a second. Didn't even blink. I brushed it off and passed it to him. He took it quick away.

"Good, huh, boy?" I said. The second cookie went by way of the first. When he was finished with that one, he eyed me, eager for more.

"That's all," I said. I raised my hands, palms out. "See." Prince stretched to my pocket and nosed it. "All gone." I turned the pocket inside out so's he could see for himself. He sniffed the seam. Gave it a few licks. When he was convinced there was no more, he sat down and looked at me. I bent down and gave him a hug. A long hug, till I was struck with a thought.

I ran to the trailer, yanked open the door, and raced to my room. I slid a shoe box from under my bed and started to head back. Before I got to the door, I was struck by another thought. Bam, like that—second one that day. I hopped to my night table and took a comb out of the top drawer. It was a sorry sight—missing so many teeth it could have posed for a jack-o'-lantern's smile. I raced back through the trailer.

"Dodi, slow down," Momma said through clenched teeth. Not that I could see—her back was turned. But I know the sound of words working their way through a tight jaw. Yes sir. I slowed. I closed the door soft.

I flew off the steps and raced back to Prince, who was waiting where I left him. I plopped down and ripped off the top of the shoe box. Inside were my paper dolls. Lots of them. They puffed, overflowing the top. I wanted to show Prince my collection.

Bet you're wondering how I came by so many. I go through Momma's magazines, after she's through reading the articles and clipping out the coupons. I cut out all the pretty ladies, tear out a house or living room. Sometimes I cut out a b-o-y, but not often.

I took one of the paper dolls and showed it to Prince. It was a movie star. She had on a red gown with sequins, hair in can-sized curls that looked soft as clouds. Prince rolled out his tongue and gave her a slurp.

"Ehhhh, no." The gown grew a wet spot. "Bad dog," I said to Prince, and wagged my finger. The way he cocked his head and looked, though, I don't believe he knew what *bad dog* meant. Then he put his nose in the box and started snuffling around, making slobber marks and wrinkles. I jerked the box away and slammed on the lid. "You're not playing nice," I told him. "Bad dog," I said. This time I made my voice go low like when Momma is at her wits' end. Prince pinned back his ears and hunkered down. He let out a whine. How can you get mad at such a pitiful creature, he seemed to be asking. And I couldn't help but loop my arms around his neck and give him a squeeze. He licked my cheek. "I guess playing paper dolls wudn't such a keen idea," I said to him.

Prince was a pretty dog 'cept his fur, and it was a tangly mess. That was why I had brought my comb outside. I got it out and started through him. The comb got stuck and pulled his hide. He let out a yip. "Ouch," I said. I know that feeling. My hair is easy to tangle, and Momma has the dickens trying to work a brush through it. Says it's like wrestling barbed wire. Sometimes she pulls so hard, I get the feeling she's going to snatch me bald. So I took the comb and ever so gentle tried dragging it through Prince's fur, but he wudn't liking it. He jerked back every time I pulled. Finally he'd had enough. He put his paw on my hand and stepped it to the ground, then lay on top of it. "Okey-dokey," I said. "I get the message. I'll leave off combing for now, but I can't have you running around looking like some moth-eaten, scraggly-hided coyote."

The rest of the morning we played fetch with the comb and hide-'n-seek, and I tried to teach Prince to sit, and shake hands, and lay down. Only when I'd say "Lay," he'd sit; and when I'd say "Sit," he'd stand; and when I'd put my hand down to shake, he'd sniff it and give me a hurt look like he was expecting another cookie. That training business was going to take some time.

CHAPTER 6

*B*y now the sun was beating down on my crown, heating it fierce. Sun was straight overhead, so it was getting along about lunch. You can tell because your shadow is round and fat and, more than likely, you're trampling it underfoot.

Just as I was about to hunt up some shade, I saw my dad rattle up in his pickup, kicking up dust. Before it had settled, he was out, striding toward the front door. He'd come home for lunch. Then, just like that, Prince zipped between my legs and headed for Daddy. Uh-oh, I said to myself, this could be trouble. With a capital T. Prince did to Daddy what he had done to Momma; he wiggled in front of Daddy's feet, dancing ever so close to those big old work boots, inches from being walloped. Less than inches, half inches, quarters. I held my breath to see what would happen—to see if my dad'd take a swipe at Prince like Momma had. Don't reckon *he'd* miss.

Only he didn't. He stopped, looked down at the whirling, twirling, turning, wiggling, twisting, dancing mop of dirty, dusty fur, and said, "What's this?" Then he squatted down and reached out to pet Prince. Prince got so excited, he jumped up and ka-chunked Daddy on the chin with the top of his head. My dad's eyes went big, but he didn't get mad. He took one of his hands and put it around Prince's neck. That hand is mighty big—I know for a fact—and it went clean around Prince's neck. He didn't do it mean, though, just firm. That made Prince sit right down and behave. Then my dad petted him with his other hand and scratched behind his ear. Daddy was talking to him low and calling him "cute little fella." Prince stuck his nose up high like he was in doggie heaven right here on earth. I could tell my dad had taken to Prince, like me, and I started to get hopeful that maybe . . .

Just then the trailer door opened wide and Momma leaned way out. "Hal." That's my dad's name. "Lunch is ready." Then she started to swing back inside, pulling the door with her; but before she got it closed, she swung out again and said, "Make Dodi get rid of that mutt. You know I don't need a dog around here to look after."

Gee whillikers. I looked down at the ground 'cause I was afraid a trickle of water might squeak out of an eye.

After I blinked away the moisture and took a deep breath, I looked up to see my dad motioning me. I shuffled over. I got this feeling I wudn't going to like what he was about to say.

"Dodi," he said as he circled my middle with his arm. He was still squatting down so we were the same size. "Where'd this dog come from?" he asked.

"Don't know, Daddy," I said. "He just 'peared out of nowhere." When Daddy didn't say anything, that set me off. "Maybe he don't got no home," I said. "Maybe he don't belong to nobody." When Daddy still didn't say anything, I charged ahead. "And if he don't belong to nobody, that means we can claim him if we want. Idn't that what that means?"

"Hold on there," he said. "Maybe he's lost. Maybe his owners are looking for him right now. Maybe they're all tore up 'cause they lost their little doggie."

"If they're all tore up," I said, "whyn't they take better care not to lose him in the first place? I would have. If I had this dog, I'd make sure he never got lost."

"Maybe," my dad said, rubbing the back of his neck, "he ran away from home."

"Why, he wouldn't run away from home unless it wudn't no good, not unless they was mean to him," I said. "And if they was mean to him, they don't deserve to own Prince. I would never be mean to him."

"Who?" Daddy asked. But before I had time to explain he said, "Never mind." He stood up. "He ain't your dog. You heard your mom." Then he said, quietlike, "You know your momma isn't too thrilled about living out here. Let's not make things worse, okay?" I didn't answer; that question was no fair.

Daddy continued, "I want you to go around the park this afternoon to see if you can find the dog's owner." When I still didn't answer, he gave me a nudge. "You hear me?"

"Yes sir," I said. I looked up. "You want me to go to every trailer in the park?" I asked.

"Yes, I do," he said. "Every trailer and camping rig. Dodi, there's not that many. It shouldn't take you long."

"What if someone's not home?" I asked.

"Well, if they're not home, I guess you can't ask then, can you?"

I shook my head. I was about to be struck with the third thought of the day.

"But"—he pointed a finger at me—"I want you to knock on every door and knock loud enough to be heard. You hear me?" he asked. It was like he was reading my thoughts.

"Mmm," I started to mumble.

"What's that?" he said.

"Yes sir," I said.

"Every spot."

"Every spot," I repeated.

"Loud," he said.

"Loud," I said back. I reckoned that was that. Daddy went inside for lunch, leaving me and Prince looking sorry-eyed at each other.

CHAPTER

7

*A*s Daddy had said, our park was purd near empty, so's I figgered I had plenty of time to find Prince's owner before Daddy got home that evening. After lunch, me and the twins played with Prince till I started casting a long shadow, telling me it was getting late—that and Momma, who yelled out the window, "What's that dog still doing here?" So I wrestled up a rope, cinched it around his neck, and off we went. Prince trotted beside me all perky, like we were going on some big adventure. That only made it worse—he had no idea what was up.

First stop was Pop Riddle's old yellow school bus. He was here when we moved in. He's been in Apache Springs a long time. That makes him a desert rat, like me. The tires on his bus have gone flat, causing it to settle in the dirt. And the dirt has blown up against it. It ain't likely that bus will be taking any more trips to school. Out front is his cactus garden. Besides collecting cactuses, Pop collects rocks. I reckon that's a holdover from his prospecting days. Amongst the prickly pear, barrel cactus, and yuccas are some interesting rocks. When I'm in the desert, if I spy a pretty one, I'll bring it back to add to his collection.

I went around to the front. Pop Riddle was lounging on the couch he keeps outside. His eyes were closed and his chin was resting on his chest. And there was his tabby cat, Babe, sprawled along the back of the couch behind Pop's head. I stopped dead in my tracks. Me and Babe don't get along so good. One time, I cornered her in Pop's cactus garden. I tried to pick her up. Just wanted to give her a friendly hug. Big mistake. That cat hauled off and swiped me across the face. I dropped her, and she shot off. But that wudn't the worst. The worst was, I lost my balance and landed on top of a prickly pear. Spent the whole afternoon with a pair of tweezers, pulling out them dern needles. Now I steer clear of Babe. Me and cats don't mix. Nosirree.

Just then Prince spied Babe. He started barking and snarling and pulling on his rope like a wild dog. I hauled back on it. "Whoa," I said. "Down, boy. You don't want to mess with that cat." Babe rose on her toes and arched her back, hissing. She's getting up in age but she's got plenty of fight left. Enough I reckon to turn one little doggie inside out. When Babe started growling and spitting, Prince went even wilder, lunging and foaming at the mouth. It was all I could do to hold him back. I believe that dog's too brave for his own good.

"Hush," Pop said, and he reached back and nudged Babe off the back of the couch. She shot out, ran under his Plymouth. Prince didn't see that. He kept his eyes peeled on the couch.

Then Pop said, "Dottie, what's that you got hold of, a werewolf?"

"Name's Dodi, Pop, not Dottie. You know that," I said. Then I added, "It's just a plain dog, Pop."

"Well, I'll be. What you doing with it, Dookie?"

"Dodi, Pop," I said, but I knew Pop knew my name. He was funning with me. "I'm taking him

46

around to find who he belongs to. Does he belong to you, Pop? Is he your dog?"

Pop sat up. "Well, bring him closer so I can take a look. How'm I suppose to tell with him clean across the yard?"

I figgered anyone can tell their dog even clear across some puny yard, but I hauled Prince over.

Pop took Prince's face in his hands. He turned his muzzle one way and studied on it, then turned it the other way. Pop closed one eye and peered down Prince's nose. He lifted a flap and inspected an ear. "Hummm," he said, "no mites, but could stand a cleaning."

Now what did that have to do with this being his dog?

Then he turned Prince all the way around and lifted his tail. Finally he looked over at me and said, "Nope, this here ain't no dog of mine." I let out a breath, which I didn't know I was holding. "But," he said to me, "I'll tell you a little secret, Toady."

"Boady. I mean Dodi. Do-di. Gee whiz, Pop, you got me so's I don't even know my own name. What secret?"

Pop leaned over and whispered, "This is one fine

dog here. Maybe not a werewolf, but a fine upstanding canine all the same. You might want to keep him yourself."

"Oh, I know, Pop. He is a fine dog, idn't he?" Pop nodded his head, brown as a walnut and just as hairless. "But I can't. Got to find his owner. Orders," I said.

Pop nodded his head again. He understood my predicament. Then he settled back on his couch, and before I could say "So long," his eyes were closed and his chin was back to resting on his chest. On to the next place.

I made my way around the park, going from trailer to trailer. Most took a quick look-see and said, "Nope, not mine. Don't know whose he is." There was a few not home. I even hit Mrs. Robinson's and the Bulldog's. Mrs. Robinson brought me out a glass of punch. Then she told me she couldn't take the dog. I kept telling her I wudn't giving Prince away, just trying to find his rightful owner. But Mrs. Robinson kept on apologizing for not being able to take him. Sometimes I wonder if Mrs. Robinson hears good.

The Bulldog was out hosing off her patio, washing off the dust. If she'd of asked me, I'd'a said that was a lost cause. But the Bulldog's mighty proud of that patio of hers. Won't let anybody skate on it or anything. She yelled at me to get off her patio before I'd even gotten to it. Then she said, "Keep that fleabag away from my yard." Geez. Well, I guessed Prince didn't belong to her neither.

Finally I got to the end of the park and noticed a little camper trailer I'd never seen before—must have moved in recently. There was a couple of cars in front I had to maneuver around. When I did, Prince commenced to strain the rope and pant. I got to the door and knocked. No answer. I turned around to leave when the door flew open. A voice boomed out, "Yes?"

That there booming voice belonged to the biggest lady I'd ever set eyes on. Almost as big as her camper. Her hair was piled atop her head and was red as a chili pepper. Looked like some of the pepper had sifted down, 'cause her cheeks were red too. She had on dangly earrings, size of poker chips. She was wearing a dress that was a field of red poppies. Holding her up were two fluffy slippers like Momma's, called mules. Guess what color? Yup— red. I knew it wudn't polite to stare, but she was an

uncommon sight in this here desert, where the sun has bleached out the color of purd near everything. And what it hasn't bleached, it's covered with dust. As my eyes worked their way back up, I noticed this here lady was holding a saucer under her chin and spooning in something yellow and soft.

Just then Prince broke loose and charged. He hopped up the pullout step to the camper and bounced off the lady's calves—big calves—and landed, *whump,* on his side in the dirt. I rushed forward and grabbed Prince around the neck. He was wiggling so much, he caused me to plop in the dirt. But that was okay, it allowed me to hug him up close and keep him from misbehaving. And I had to hug him tight 'cause he was squirming around, trying to break loose and charge again.

I said, "Don't know what's gotten into him. Prince is a good dog. He never done that before. He never jumped on anyone before. And me and him, we been to every trailer in this here park, hunting up his owner, but we haven't found him yet, have we, boy? Which is okay by us. Yessirree. 'Cause if we don't find his owner then that means that maybe I can keep him for my very own." Whew. I said a mouthful that time. I looked up at the huge lady.

She didn't say anything. She was squinting at us like she was pondering something. I was thinking maybe she couldn't talk when she took a deep breath and said, "Maybe he's hungry." Then she turned sideways and stepped down to the pullout step, real slow. The little camper groaned and sagged. When she stepped onto the ground, the camper groaned and rose back up, like an accordion. She lowered herself down, her tent dress billowing out, and placed the saucer on the ground. She did this real slow too. Before she had time to raise up, Prince broke loose, ran over to her, jumped up—placing a dusty paw on her dress—and started to lick her face.

"Muffy, cut that out," she said. She pushed him away with one of those arms, bigger around than my leg, bigger around than Momma's leg, both Momma's legs. She didn't push hard, but it landed Prince by the saucer. As soon as he spied it, he dug in. Which, close as I could figger, had in it banana pudding.

"Muffy?" I said. "Is that what you called him? His name's not Muffy. It's Prince."

"Oh, sorry," she said. "I guess I misunderstood. Prince is a fine name."

"Suits him, doesn't it? Course, right now he could use some sprucing up. But even so, you can tell he's got good bloodlines. He might even be a thoroughbred. Don't you think?"

I heard a giggle, though I didn't know what I said was funny. "Sure," she said. "So," she continued, "you say you plan on keeping this dog if you can't find his owner?" Before I could answer, she said, "I'll bet you'll take real good care of him, won't you?"

"Oh yes," I said.

"Keep him fed, plenty of water. Give him a walk every day. He likes to go for walks."

"He does?" I asked. How do you reckon she knew that?

"All dogs do," she answered in response to my question, which I was thinking but hadn't got around to asking.

"Oh."

Prince was licking the saucer clean. As he did, the saucer scooted across the hardscrabble dirt, and as it scooted, Prince walked forward, never missing a lick.

The fat lady said, "Just a minute." She turned and squeezed back inside her trailer. She came out holding a small leather collar. "Here." She tossed it my way. "You might as well have this." It was scuffed, but it was better than a scratchy rope. Plus it fit Prince perfect.

"Well," said the fat lady. "It's too hot out here for me. I'm going back inside and park it under the AC. Only way to keep cool in this heat." With that, she turned and went inside the trailer.

"Here, ma'am," I said before she shut the door. I handed her the saucer.

"You take good care of that dog," she told me.

"Oh, I surely will. Be seeing you around, I guess," I said as I patted my leg for Prince to come.

"Nope, you won't," she said. "Soon as my old man gets home, we're heading out. I've taken as much of this flyspeck as I can stand." Then she disappeared inside her camper, and I was left staring at the door.

"C'mon, Prince," I said. Time for us to be heading out too. Heading for home, that is. But Prince didn't move. He was staring at the door. "C'mon, boy," I said. When he still didn't budge, I went and took ahold of the collar and gave it a tug while I tried to coax him along. Only he wudn't coaxing. "What's the matter with you? You still hungry?" I asked. "I'll rustle you up something when we get home." That must have been it, because all of a sudden Prince gave in and fell in step behind me. Off we trotted.

"Uh-oh." I stopped cold, causing Prince to plow into the back of one knee. After all that, I'd plumb forgot to ask that lady if this was her dog. Well, shoot; I reckoned she would have said so during all that time if he was. Right? And off we trotted again. Then it dawned on me—that was the last spot. I'd gone through the whole park—to every spot that was occupied—and not one person laid claim to my Prince. Yippee!

I reached our yard the same time Daddy drove up. He pulled in, kicking up dust. "Daddy," I said. "Daddy, Daddy, Daddy."

"Whatie?" he answered.

I ran up to him, bouncing up and down like a jumping bean. Daddy put a hand on each shoulder to settle me down like he'd done to Prince early on.

"Daddy," I said again. "I been to every place in the park, and Prince don't belong to nobody."

"Every place?" he asked. "Even . . ." And Daddy nodded his head in the direction of the Bulldog's. She lives behind us, so our yards line up, except her trailer faces toward the blacktop and ours the other way.

"Yes sir," I said, "even . . ." And I nodded in her direction like Daddy.

"Well," said my dad, "looks like somebody dumped this fella."

"What do you mean, dumped?"

"I mean," he said, "someone was traveling through." He waved his arm in the direction of the blacktop. "They pulled over to the side of the road, set him out of the car, and took off down the highway."

"But why'd they do that?" Why would anyone dump a great little dog like this? It didn't make me no sense.

"'Cause they're no good. Should be shot," he mumbled. "Dog could die of thirst in sight of two days in this desert."

"Well, it's a good thing we're here so he won't, huh, Dad?"

"What?"

"I say . . ."

"Now Dodi, nobody said you could keep this dog. You heard what your momma said—she doesn't want a dog around here."

"But Daddy, what can we do? If we don't look after him, he'll die. You said so. Daddy? Daddy?" Panic was setting in. I glanced down at Prince. He shifted his feet and gave out a whimper: *Mmmmm.*

"We can find him a home, that's what we can do," Daddy said.

"Gee whillikers."

"Hey," he said sharp, and pointed a finger at me. "None of that now. You remember what your mom'd said. She isn't going to allow any dog around here. You knew that. You knew that dog wasn't going to stay. Right? . . . Right?" he said again, louder, when I didn't answer.

"Yes sir," I mumbled into my chest.

My dad started toward the trailer. Then he stopped and turned back to me. "He can stay till you find him a new home. That's all."

"Hal," said Momma. She had stuck her head out of the trailer when she heard Daddy drive up and was listening to our exchange.

"Just until she finds him a home. What harm can it do?" Daddy said to her.

Momma set her jaw and disappeared inside the trailer.

"Till I find him a *good* home," I said to Daddy.

"Sure, a good home."

"With a little girl," I said. "Prince is partial to girls."

Daddy let out a sigh. "If you can. In the meantime, you got to take care of him, you hear?"

"Yes sir."

"Keep him out of mischief."

"Yes sir."

"I mean it. If you don't, I take that dog straight to Fort Bennett, to the animal shelter."

Oh no. I didn't want Prince to end up in no animal shelter. The dogs that go in there don't all come out. Most don't get adopted. I knew that.

But I tried to think positive. I mean, just how much trouble can one little dog get into? I soon found out. A bunch. Yessirree.

"Now let's go inside—find that little guy a water dish and some grub," said Daddy.

CHAPTER

8

*S*o that was how I came by Prince, but that's not the end of my story. No way. I made up my mind to enjoy him while I had him and not think on him leaving. Besides, I figgered, maybe I could drag out finding him a home.

First thing I did as Prince's new owner was give him a bath. I soaked him with the hose, lathered him with Ivory—careful around his eyes—and rinsed him off. And while I was doing this, Prince was giving me a bath too. Me and the twins, 'cause they were watching this production. Every time he'd shake and fling water, they'd squeal and clap their hands, which only made him shake more.

Then I dried everyone off. I tried to comb him again. No way, he said. So I cut the snarls and cockleburs out of his fur with Momma's manicure scissors. I caught what-for for that.

Did I say I couldn't imagine what trouble one little dog could get into? Well, I found out *real* soon.

First thing, Prince barked a lot. A whole lot. Seemed any little thing would set him off—a car driving by, a tumbleweed skittering across the yard, and if he spotted Pop's tabby, plug your ears 'cause Prince was about to let loose with a yapfest, or as Momma would say, a nerve-wracking din. When that happened, she'd put her hand across her forehead and roll her eyes upward. I knew to get outside quick and make Prince shut his yapper.

Second thing, that little dog could dig. Whenever I had to go inside, Prince was apt to crawl under the trailer and spoon out a hole to get at the cool dirt below. He'd lay there till I came out to play. He had four or five such holes going when Dad spied a mound of dirt by the stack of blocks that the trailer hitch rests on. The blocks keep the trailer from tipping forward like a teeter-totter when we all pile to the front. Daddy got some kind of mad about that, said he didn't need for our trailer to tip over some night. So me, I crawled underneath and filled in the holes. Next time I came out of the house, there was Prince digging up one of my filled-in holes. So I picked out a spot in the shade by the propane tank and dampened it down and helped Prince dig him another hole. I kept it damp, but not muddy, so's Prince had a cool place to rest anytime he wanted.

Third thing, Prince was death on toys or shoes or anything left within his reach. I gave him a holey sock to play with and one of Daddy's old work boots to gnaw but that didn't make no never mind. We'd leave anything outside, it was going to get chewed. Prince nibbled away the heel on one of my flip-flops. But it was still serviceable. The twins' toy gun had its barrel reduced to a nub. But the worst was the stuffed bear. Worst because it was their favorite toy, and worst because there wudn't nothing left of that bear time Prince got through with it. Nothing 'cept scraps of fluff and dirty stuffing all over our yard and yonder into the Bulldog's.

When I seen what he'd done, I grabbed half a bear leg—half was all that was left—and shook it in Prince's face, and said, "This ain't yours, it's the twins'. You leave off stuff that don't belong to you. You hear?" In response, Prince jumped up and grabbed one end of that leg and started to growl and tug like it was some kind of game I was about.

During this time, the twins had come toddling over. When it dawned on them what I had in my hand, they both let out screeching that set my ears to ringing and my eyes to watering. See, they thought Mr. Ted E. Bear was real, and seeing his innards helter-skelter was a shock. Couldn't say I blamed them.

Well, all that racket made the Bulldog poke her nose out between her kitchen curtains. When she saw the bear filling ringing her patio like bathtub scum, she came stomping out her door. Same time, Jesse came clomping out our door. To stick his nose into what didn't concern him.

Anyway, Jesse had a front-row seat when the Bulldog came across her patio to our yard, a wagging finger leading the charge. "Look at this messsssss," she said, showering me with *s*'s. She put a death grip on my arm and jerked me toward her yard. Jerked me right out of my flip-flops. I skittered over the rocks—*ouch, ouch, ouch.*

"I expect you to clean this up, little lady. Pronto," she said. "Every last bit."

"Yes ma'am," I said.

"And you keep that dog in your own yard. I got no use for dogs messing up my property."

"How do you know he was on your property?" I asked. "How do you know this stuff didn't blow over here by itself?"

Her mouth narrowed to two thin lines. "Did your dog make this mess or didn't he?"

"Well," I said, "I didn't exactly see him do it." And I didn't truly, though I reckon he was the odds-on favorite.

"Are you sassing me?" she asked, and pinched down on my arm, hard enough to stop blood flowing.

"No ma'am," I said. Then I added, for good measure, "And I'll clean up this here mess. Every last bit."

"You bet you will." She let go of my arm with one last twist and marched back to her trailer.

The only good thing that'd come of that, the twins had quieted down when she'd made her appearance. They're young but already realize the Bulldog is to be avoided at all cost.

Jesse had taken off too. Gee, it wudn't like him to miss a run-in with the Bulldog, especially if it involved you know who.

But then the trailer door opened and out he came, leading Momma, who was drying her hands on a dish towel. Momma surveyed the bear gut-strewed yard, then me, then the twins. I didn't need to explain a thing to her—she knew what had happened just by the evidence and, of course, Jesse's big mouth. Momma lit into me with a scolding. She ended by letting me know if I couldn't make that dog behave, then she was going to have Daddy get rid of him. Did she make herself clear? And how. Then she turned and went back inside and slammed the door shut.

"Face it, Dodi," said Jesse. "That dog's days are numbered."

"Oh, what do you know anyway," I said as I started to pick up bear guts.

"Nobody wants that mangy dog around here," he said. "That mutt's always rolling in the dirt, he's got fleas, and he's got doggie breath. He's a mess. And he's ugly."

"He is not and he does not." Well, he maybe had

doggie breath, but, geez, he was a doggie. And, anyway, you get used to it. "I want him, and the twins want him," I said. "That's three that wants him."

"Momma don't want him, and Daddy don't want him," he said. "And they count for a lot more than you and those half-pints."

"Aww," I said. I tried to think of something smart to say back, but I couldn't right off. He wudn't wrong. "Aww, go play with Dickey Martin," I said, "and leave us alone."

"My pleasure," he said, and off he trotted.

I continued picking up bear. As I picked up Mr. Ted E. Bear, I put him in the twins' wagon. When I got him collected, I'd throw the caboodle in the trash. We collect our garbage in a drum sitting back of our trailer. When it gets full, me and Daddy and Jesse take it to the dump.

The twins toddled over to see what I was doing. They were slapping around the bear fluff when suddenly it dawned on them—for the second time—what it was balled in their fists. Then they went "Uhf, uhf, uhf" as they sucked in air, then "Eeeeeeeeeeee" as they let it out.

I could think of only one thing to do to shut them up. I went lickety-split into the trailer to grab my paper doll box. I took off the lid to let them play in it and hoped there'd be something left by the time I could wheedle it away.

If you think that was the end of the bear fiasco— no way. When Daddy drove up later for lunch, Jesse appeared out of nowhere and ran up to spill the beans again. I took a gander at Prince, took a deep breath, and got ready for another bawling out, or worse. Instead Daddy didn't even look my way. He said to Jesse, "Did I ask you about that?"

Jesse said, "No sir." He said it quiet, like he was shrunk into himself. Then Daddy turned and went into the trailer.

CHAPTER

9

A couple of days later, me and Prince was taking us a stroll at the dump. The dump is a big gully where people dump their junk, like it's called. It's a neat place to scout—sometimes you can find wood scraps for fort-making or toys not too far gone. Also it's fun clambering over the car shells, providing you don't slip and get skewered on a rusty bolt. No one has to torch the trash 'cause it sets itself afire under the hot sun. Honest. All by itself. Only then the sun wudn't out. The clouds had roiled up like an ugly bruise. Most times they put on a good show, then dissolve without shaking loose a drop. But not that day. That day they let loose a torrent—a gully-washer. Sudden. Me and Prince tore toward home.

We was racing along—me in the lead—when we rounded the Bulldog's trailer. I circled wide. But Prince, fixing to head me off, cut across her patio. He peeled around the add-on room built on her back door. I looked over my shoulder at the muddy paw prints streaking her cement. But gosh, the way it was pouring down, I figgered they'd wash away in no time. They was already melting to light tan. Turns out I figgered wrong.

That evening, just as we were sitting down to dinner, here comes the Bulldog, banging on our trailer. *Bang! Bang! Bang!* Daddy barely got the door open when she started in, "Mr. Tanner." That's my dad. "You better do something about that dog," she said.

"Mizz Bullock," my dad said. That's the Bulldog's name, like I told you before. "What's the matter now?" he asked. He let out a sigh. They'd had dealings before. Usually about us kids. I was closest to the door, so I could hear what was being said over the din of the swamp cooler. Not Jesse. He was clean across the other side and was straining to hear,

but couldn't. Momma was shoveling food into the twins and wudn't paying the Bulldog any mind, at first.

"That mutt of yours was in my yard," she said. "Tracked up my patio. If I wanted to spend my days cleaning up after a dog, I'd have one. But I don't. And I'm sure not going to clean up after yours, you hear me?"

"I hear you," Daddy said.

"If you don't believe me," she went, "just ask your kid, that Dodi."

"Oh, I believe you, but no use blowing a gasket over a little mud."

When he said that, her face flushed red, her cheeks blew out. *Sputter, sputter, sputter,* she went. "I'll do more than blow a gasket. I'll shoot me a dog, it does that again."

"Now hold on a min—" started Daddy, but before he could get any more out, she'd spun around and marched off. By this time Momma had looked up and had her ear tuned toward the door.

Then he turned to me. "Dodi . . . ," he said.

"Daddy, is she going to shoot Prince?" I said. Panic was rising up. My heart was thumping *thumpity-thump, thumpity-thump*—like that. Like a jackrabbit caged up inside, hitting with his feet, trying to get out. Prince is fast, but no way could he outrun a bullet. My mind conjured up an image. A horrible image of little Prince running, running as fast as he could, looking over his shoulder, terrified at what he saw. At that Bulldog taking aim, then *blam,* and Prince tumbling over and over and over. He comes to rest on the hard ground. He tries to get up but he can't. He whimpers. He don't understand. He doesn't know about guns. He doesn't understand why someone would hurt him. He wonders why I can't make the hurt go away. But I can't. I can't do nothing but watch him suffer. Then . . .

I screamed, "Daddy, the Bulldog is gonna shoot Prince!" Now my heart was pounding—*boom, boom, boom*—like that. Like cannons going off in my chest.

"No, Dodi," he said, "she's not going to shoot Prince."

"But she said . . . she said she was gonna shoot him. I heard her." I was jumping up and down. "I heard her. She's gonna shoot my dog. Why would she do that? Why would she shoot a little doggie? He didn't mean no harm. He's my friend. He's the only friend I got. In the whole world. Why would she do that?" I was screaming the words. My cheeks were wet.

"Dodi, hush," said Momma.

Daddy wrapped his arms around me. "Shhh," he said. "She's just talking. Dodi, don't you worry. Nobody's going to shoot your dog." That calmed me some. I had gotten quiet and stopped jumping, but my innards were still flip-flopping.

"I swear," said Momma, "that woman is just awful. Imagine saying that in front of a child." To tell you the truth, ain't no one in my family on good terms with the Bulldog. We've all had ugly words with her.

It took a while, but finally I had calmed down enough so my dad felt it was safe to unwrap his arms. "Dodi," he said, "since you've finished your supper . . ." Then he added with a sigh, "More or less. You go on outside and keep an eye on Prince while me and your momma talk."

Jesse made bug eyes at me and started to snicker.

Daddy turned to Jesse. "You go too."

"Why do I got to go outside?" Jesse whined.

"Because I say," said Daddy.

"But I didn't do nothing." Whine.

"Out," said Dad, and pointed to the door. Jesse shuffled out the door after me and stomped down the steps.

As soon as we got outside, Jesse said, "Well, Dodi, better say bye-bye to that dumb *dog*." He yelled out *dog* and lunged at Prince. But Prince jumped out of the way. Then Prince started running around in a circle, barking and snarling at Jesse, and I had to run over and put my hand over his snout to shush him, but not before Daddy opened the door and said, "Dodi, keep that dog quiet."

Old Jesse thought that was funny. He started laughing, "Hah, hah, hah." He'd gotten my dog in trouble at a time when Prince needed to be on his superspecial best behavior. He made me so mad, I could've chewed rawhide. "Better say good-bye to your dog, Dodi, 'cause he's good as gone," he said.

I decided to ignore that last comment. "I taught Prince a new trick," I said.

"Humph." He shrugged, like he wudn't interested. "What?" he finally asked. Jesse'll never learn when to keep his mouth shut.

"I taught him to git people. People I don't like."

"Oh yeah," he said. "That dog couldn't get a tin can if he was tied to it."

I knelt beside Prince and encircled his neck with my arms. I leaned in close to his ear and whispered, "Babe."

Soon as I did, Prince perked to attention. I got him looking Jesse's way. I whispered "Babe" again. Prince let out a growl deep in his throat. Jesse started fidgeting.

Jesse didn't look 100 percent convinced that my two skinny arms could keep him from being dog chewy. I whispered to Prince, "Where's the cat?" That set Prince to snarling. He was struggling against me. He curled his lips, showing fangs. He put on a good show.

Jesse said, "He don't scare me." But I noticed he was backing up. He backed clean out of our yard. "I'm going to visit Dickey," he said, then turned and skedaddled.

At first I felt full of myself that me and Prince made Jesse turn tail. But that was soon reduced to

half full, then quarter, then not enough to spit on—
I could hear Momma and Daddy inside the trailer,
talking over the fate of my dog.

I didn't know what I'd do if they said Prince had
to go. Jesse had Dickey Martin, but I didn't have me
one decent friend to play with. I'd had me Josie
Lopez, but her and her mom pulled out right before
school was out. So now all I had was Prince and my
paper dolls, and you can't play tug-of-war with a
paper doll or fetch or go for walks or snuggle up to,
like you can a dog.

Besides, where would Prince go? Didn't anybody
claim him. And if'n we could find someone to take
him in, how would they treat him? Would they know
how to scratch behind his ears like he liked or feed
him crème-filled sandwich cookies or take him for
walks at the dump? Would they have a girl for
him to play with, or would they keep little Prince
chained up outside all day, panting in the hot sun?
And what if we couldn't find someone to take him
in? Then Dad would take him to Fort Bennett, to
the animal shelter. I heard what they do to dogs
nobody wants—they put them to sleep. The sleep
they don't wake from. I gave Prince a long hug, hop-

ing to chase them ugly thoughts from my mind. One thing for sure: if Daddy and Momma said Prince had to go, I was going to pitch a fit like they never saw, and I didn't care how hard a licking I got.

I was hugging Prince, working myself up, when Daddy came out. He came over and squatted beside us and started petting Prince. Prince put his nose in the air and lidded his eyes and relaxed against Daddy's leg. Poor Prince—Dad was about to sentence him to death row for dogs, and he was mooching him up like he didn't know from nothing—which he didn't.

Daddy took a deep breath and gave me a long look. Real long. I wanted to scream, I was about to bust. Whyn't he just blurt it out and be done with. But he surprised me. Did he ever.

Daddy said, "Me and your momma decided you can keep your dog."

"Oh, Daddy," I said. I was so happy, I didn't know if I was going to laugh or cry. Then I hugged Prince so hard I made him yip. "Oh, fella, I'm sorry," I said. That set me off. I started to cry, and then I started to laugh. Idn't that peculiar—to laugh and cry, both at the same time.

But my dad wudn't finished. "On one condition."

"What?" I asked, not sure I wanted to hear. I knew it was just too good to be true—there was bound to be a catch.

"You, little missy, have got to keep him tied up," he said. "We can't have him running loose, causing grief to the neighbors."

I thought about that a minute, then said, "But, Daddy, I don't believe Prince will take to being tied up." See, Prince had never been tied up before. He was used to his freedom. Also, I wudn't sure Prince had come to the full realization he was a dog, so I didn't believe he'd cotton being treated like one.

"It doesn't matter whether he takes to it or not. You keep him tied up and out of mischief or he goes. Is that clear?"

"Even when I'm outside with him, Dad? I'll keep an eye on him then. I promise I will. It doesn't seem right he's got to be tied up all the time."

Daddy sighed and looked past me. Gulp. Uh-oh, maybe I said too much. Maybe I should have kept my mouth shut while I had me a victory. Could be I got as big a mouth as Jesse.

My dad said, "No. I don't want an argument about this. You can take him for walks, but when you're home, that dog stays chained. You got to keep him out of trouble. Your momma isn't about to suffer any more run-ins with the neighbors, no more chewed toys or shoes, or a yard that looks like the dump. If Prince messes up one more time, if the Bulldog—er, Mizz Bullock—or anyone comes over to complain again, that dog will have to go. Now that's all I'm going to say on the subject." And with that he stood up. "Well, let's see if I can scrounge up something to keep this fella under control."

Daddy walked over and rummaged in the truck bed and came back with a chain. He hooked it through the front step. Then he took a rope, cut off a piece, and looped it through Prince's collar. He fastened the rope to the chain. It was pretty long. Long enough so Prince had the run of half the yard and could get under the trailer into the shade.

Just as I suspected, Prince didn't take to being tied, no way. First time he tried to trot after me, he ran out of chain and got pulled up short. He whirled around to see who had ahold of him and gave the chain a sniff. Then he commenced to pull and yank but, of course, the chain held fast. He swiped at it with his paw, which made his head jerk. Finally he got tuckered out and lay down, panting. So I thought, Well, that's that. But before long he'd forgotten he was tied and took off again. The chain snapped him back, landing him on his back. *Thud* into the dirt. Hard. That made him mad. He turned around and bit the chain. He spit it out fast— *ptooey*—and shook his head. That made me feel bad. I knelt down beside him and worked my fingers up under his collar and rubbed his neck where the leather had bit into the skin. I explained the business about the chain, how it was for his own good. Don't know if he understood, though.

I tried to stay around the steps to keep him company, but I couldn't all the time. I had chores to do and the twins to wagon-push. After a few days, Prince figured out just how far that chain would allow him to go. So when he ran after us, he knew the exact instant to pull up so's the chain wouldn't jerk him off his feet. Then the poor little fellow would watch all eager at the end of his tether and whine. But better this than you know what.

CHAPTER

10

A couple of days later, I had just gotten back from taking Prince on a walk when I spied Mrs. Robinson in her yard. All around Mrs. Robinson's cinder-block house is grass and trees and all manner of bushes and flowers. Not like ours with no trees and hardpan dirt. Momma said Mr. Robinson carted in truckloads of dirt from the mountains so's she could have her yard. Momma tried to grow grass in our yard, but it didn't take. Daddy offered to cart in dirt too, but Momma said no, hoped we wouldn't be staying. We're still here, though. That's because Daddy has a steady job at the gas station. And it's hard to give up a steady job when there's six mouths to feed. That's what Daddy says. Mr. Robinson also built Mrs. Robinson her house. Momma said it was the only way Mrs. Robinson would agree to live here. Trailer living idn't her style.

Her house is off by itself, but I can see it from our yard because there is an empty patch between our trailer and her place. She was on her knees, working in her yard behind her fence. I'm not suppose to bother Mrs. Robinson, but after a few minutes she looked up, and saw me, and waved. I waved back. She stood up, and went up to her fence, and waved me over. Whoopee, I love it at Mrs. Robinson's. I raced over. After all, that wudn't bothering her. Not since she waved me over.

When I got to Mrs. Robinson's, she invited me inside her house. I kicked off my shoes at her door so's not to track up her carpet. She's got carpet over every bit of floor except the kitchen. Momma said she doesn't see how she can keep it clean with all the dust, but it looked clean to me. It looked brand-new. It's blue as the sky and fun to sit on—it tickles my bare legs. But I didn't sit on it that day. I went into the kitchen for some Kool-Aid and sugar cook-ies—homemade, with pink frosting. The cookies were hard, but I didn't tell Mrs. Robinson that. I just didn't ask for seconds.

Then I went into the living room and played her white piano. I didn't really play. I plunked out the notes, one at a time, to see if I could make a song. Couldn't. Leastways not one you'd recognize. Mrs. Robinson busied herself around her house like I wudn't there, so I reckoned I still wudn't bothering her. Even so, I got up to go after a while. Didn't want to wear out my welcome, as Momma would say. I thanked her for the cookies and Kool-Aid, and she said, "You're very welcome, Dodi." Then I left. I was careful to shut the door soft.

When I reached down to slip on my shoes, I got a face full of fur. Prince had followed me over. He was yipping at me, nipping at my shorts and shirttail, and bouncing off my legs, all wound up. But how'd he get in? Her place is fenced in, and the gate was latched.

Uh-oh. Over to one side, on a beeline to our trailer, was fresh-turned earth. That Prince had dug under Mrs. Robinson's fence. But that wudn't the worst. My eyes bounced around the yard. Rocks lined bark-covered paths that looped around carpets of different-colored flowers: orange and blue and red and bubble-gum pink. All those bright colors smack-dab in the middle of the desert. Coming over to Mrs. Robinson's was like being Dorothy in Oz. My eyes were roving around the yard when I seen it—in the middle of the bubble-gum flowers was an ugly brown bare spot. It didn't take me but a second to realize Prince had dug himself another cool-off hole. Littering the path, lying on their sides like fallen soldiers, were dozens of massacred pink posies. It was more than a body could bear. I let out a shriek and tore off toward home, Prince hot on my heels and yipping all happylike, not knowing the terrible, the double-terrible, the triple-terrible thing he'd done.

I ran to the far side of my tank, to the old Prince, the good Prince, the Prince that didn't dig up nice ladies' flower gardens. I sat in the dirt, never mind the rocks, and put my head in my hands and wished for it to be morning again, so what happened wouldn't have. But it didn't work. Every time I tried to go back in time, I'd feel a nudge on my hands. A cold wet nudge. When I'd peek out, I'd see two marbly eyes looking at me and a tail starting up. I'd

close my eyes tight and try harder. There it would go again—nudge. And there would be those two eyes, merry rascally eyes, looking at me.

"Go away," I said to Prince. "Go away. You're a bad dog." But he didn't go. His eyes weren't as merry now and his tail'd stopped, but he stayed put. "Go," I said, ugly and mean. "You're a worthless, no-account, troublemaker, no-good dog. You hear me? So just git." But he still didn't go. His eyes weren't merry at all now, but he stayed put.

"I said, *Go*," I yelled at him and shot my foot out, kicking him in the chest. This time he jumped up and let out a yip, more from surprise than hurt, I 'spect. Then I buried my face again and drew up my knees and stayed like that for a long time.

Finally I had to move—my rear'd gone numb and legs were achy. So I peeled myself apart. I looked around for Prince. I didn't see him. That was strange, 'cause Prince was always right there whenever I was outside, like we were Siamese twins, like we were buddies, which we were—best buddies. Then I remembered that I was mean to Prince. I'd lost my temper and kicked him. You don't suppose he could of run off, do you?

"PRINCE!!" I screamed, loud as I could. Before I caught my next breath, I was eating fur. Prince must have been on the other side of the tank, 'cause he came lickety-split. He was so excited, so glad that I didn't mean for him to go for real, he started wiggling this way and that, tap dancing between my legs, on my legs. *Oooo*, sharp nails. When he finally wore himself out, he stood back, ears at attention, eyes bright and rascally again. Happy as the twins at chow time or me with new sneakers or Momma when she gets a letter from home.

"Now what?" I asked him. "When Mrs. Robinson comes over and tattles on you, tells Momma that you ruined her beautiful flowers, that's it. Momma said if she has to hear one more person complain, one more person get mad because of you, that's it. Maybe Momma and Daddy would overlook that mean Bulldog getting upset again. After all, she *is* the Bulldog. It's awful tough keeping on her good side, no matter how hard you try. But not nice Mrs. Robinson. With the pretty yard. That she spends hours and hours working in, making it perfect. When she comes over and tells that you ruined it, they won't overlook that." I took his head between my hands and looked into his eyes. *"Adiós,"* I said. I wanted to know how it was going to feel when the time came. It felt awful. *"Adiós, mi amigo. Adiós,* little Prince."* It only got worse the more I said it. Soon I couldn't say anything at all. The words stuck in my throat and wouldn't come out.

That night I couldn't sleep. I tossed and turned this way and that, thinking about Prince's fate. The worst part was, it was my fault. After our walk, I had forgotten to tie him up, like I was suppose to. Like I promised I would. That's how come he was able to follow me over to Mrs. Robinson's and dig under her fence and tear up her flowers. And the next time Mrs. Robinson goes out to her flower garden and discovers the damage Prince done, and comes over and tells Momma, my dog is as good as gone. To Fort Bennett. To that animal shelter. And it was my fault. My fault. My fault.

CHAPTER

11

*M*orning finally put in an appearance. I was wide awake lying in bed, waiting for everyone to start stirring. Finally I got up and went outside. Prince was still asleep. I went over and knelt down and stroked his head. He didn't open his eyes, just swallowed a couple of times. He trusted me. Knew I'd never hurt him. That shows you how wrong he was; I turned out to be his worst enemy.

"You're a good dog, Prince," I said to him. "You're the best dog anyone could ever want. Yessirree." I stayed outside, petting him awhile. The trailer was quiet—it was Sunday. It was still early, the air was cool. Mr. Sun was just starting to show his face.

Prince loved his walks so much, I said, "We'll go for another walk this morning, before anyone gets up." He perked up with the mention of *walk*. "Walkie, Prince. Walkie." His tail started up. And I knew just the place. We were going to the top of Little Toad. Then I was going to cross over to Big Toad and slide down Satan's slide. Just like Jesse and Dickey Martin had done. And I'd go now before Mom woke up and asked me where I was going, and then tell me I couldn't go because I was too little, and then I'd have to listen to Jesse laugh, and then I'd have to sit around waiting for Mrs. Robinson to come marching over, and then I'd have to watch Prince be driven to Fort Bennett to the animal shelter. If there was ever a day that called for courage to climb Little Toad, this was it. After all, what did I have to lose?

I ran back inside the trailer, threw on my clothes and a pair of sneakers. I rolled up a couple of peanut butter and jelly tortillas and stuffed them in an empty bread bag along with an apple and a handful of crème-filled sandwich cookies. I filled my school thermos with water. Then I went outside to undo Prince. Hmm. I went back inside and left a note telling Momma that me and Prince went hiking so she wouldn't worry. Then I went back outside, tied Prince to a rope, and we were off. We crossed the highway and started the slow rise to Little and Big Toad. Couldn't say how far away they were, but I knew we had a good hour of walking. And that was just to get to the base of Little Toad. Then we had us a steep climb over some tricky rocks.

Soon as I crossed the highway, I untied Prince to let him run. Away he went, nose to the ground, tail up. I didn't worry about losing him, though, 'cause every five minutes he'd stop, raise his head, and look back to make sure I was coming. Sometimes he'd come all the way back to my side and walk with me for a short piece, then off he'd go again.

All of a sudden, I heard him take off, yipping. I started running to see what had set him off. What I saw was a furry hiney sticking up. His front part was hunkered down amongst the rocks. His ears were flip-flopping, up and down, in time to his paws, which were scratching the dirt for all they were worth. He was flinging dirt right and left. Some of it slapped my legs and fell on my sneakers.

What he'd done was chased some critter—probably a lizard—down a hole, and he was bent on

digging that sucker out. Desert dirt is cement hard and full of rocks, but he didn't pay it no mind. Every minute or so, he'd stick his snout down the hole and snort. Sure hoped he didn't have some sidewinder down there. Finally he stopped, backed up a bit, looked at me as if to say, What are you doing standing around for? I took a stick and poked at the hole. Prince watched for a minute, then nudged me out of the way and started digging and scratching again.

The sun was beating down, and I was heating up. Besides, we needed to get going if we aimed to get all the way to the top of Little Toad. "C'mon, Prince," I said, and I patted my leg. "You're going to wear yourself out. Besides, I'll bet that lizard's already scooted out his back door. He's probably watching and laughing at your foolishness." But Prince kept at it, flinging dirt. I started to walk away. "You can stay here if you want, but I'm leaving." He didn't look up. "I say, *I'm leaving*," I shouted at him, and stomped off.

I went a ways and looked back. He was still at it. "You don't believe me, but I'm leaving you. See, here I go," I yelled. He didn't even glance my way. I walked on some more. Now when I turned to look, he wudn't in sight. I whistled and shouted for him. Nothing.

I turned around and walked back. When he came within eyesight, I saw he was still at the hole. It was bigger, but not by much. "Prince, you come here right now," I said, like I meant business. But he didn't. I had to go all-l-l the way back, take him around the neck, and drag him away. And Momma says I'm stubborn.

We walked on some more. By now it was fiercely hot. Hot enough to make blue lakes up ahead. Only no use running after them—I know—because soon as you get to where one is, it's gone. See, they're mirages; they ain't really real.

By now Prince was walking beside me—he'd wore himself out. His pink tongue was hanging out the side of his mouth, about as far as I reckoned he could hang it. So I stopped and unscrewed my thermos. I poured some water in the lid and set it down for Prince, then took a couple of swigs out of the bottle. I made sure Prince had his fill, then I sprinkled some on his head and over his back—to help cool him off. I dribbled some on my arms and legs while I was at it. I took out one of my tortillas and started to eat it while I walked. Prince danced around underfoot, backwards, so he could watch every bite, nose high to catch a whiff of peanut butter. That dog loves to eat, maybe more than the twins. I believe if a jackrabbit were to have crossed our path right then, he wouldn't have given it a glance. Every third bite, I'd tear off a piece and toss it to him.

We wound our way through a stand of mesquite. I had to be on the lookout—this was where the big kids came to sneak cigarettes. But I didn't see anyone. I didn't see anyone or anything the rest of the way, unless you count a couple of lizards that darted across our path. This was the desert, and the desert is a sparse place. It seemed like those mountains took forever to reach. But finally we were there.

I was down to the apple and half a thermos of water, which I put in the shade of a boulder for safekeeping. Then I started climbing. I didn't climb straight up. That would have been too hard. I went catty-whompus across Little Toad, making my way higher a bit at a time. That way when I reached Big Toad, what has Satan's slide, I'd only have to go a little ways before I'd be at the top of the slide. Then I'd sit down and go. In case you're still confused about what exactly Satan's slide *is*, I was fixing to go down, I'll tell you. It's like a slide at the playground, only it's steeper, and longer, and scarier. It ain't for little kids. And instead of smooth metal, you scoot on loose gravel and sand. If it sounds painful, it ain't. Leastways, I hoped not. Satan's slide's been worn smooth by the backsides of hundreds, maybe thousands, of kids over the years. It will do a number on your jeans, though. Just ask Jesse. So I had worn my sorriest cutoffs. They were so patched, one more wouldn't matter.

There was one tricky part to the climb: it was a drop-off three-quarters of the way up; and when I got to it, I had an argument with myself—did I really need to go to the very tippy top, or should I be content to pick my way to the slide from here? But I figgered I'd gone this far, I might as well go all the way. The drop-off was about kid-high, which may not sound too high, lessen you're a kid. I moved along it until I found me a place with a couple of sticking-out rocks that I could use as steps and handholds. First, though, I picked Prince up and lifted him, *oomph,* over the top.

Then I started up it. I put one knobby knee south and the other one north, elbows out, rear waving in the breeze, and nose dusting dirt. Then pinching rocks with my fingers, I edged up. I slipped and caught my chin on an outcropping. I left it there—I could use another hold. Let me tell you, I felt like a discombobulated spider. And I knew, one slip and I'd be a goner—I'd tumble down the mountain, not stopping till I hit bottom.

But, not to worry, I managed to pull myself over the top. I rolled over and lay flat out. I stayed that way a long time—till my heart stopped pounding. Then I lay there some more. After a while Prince came over and stared down at me. He was panting. He plopped down by my side, put his head on his paws, and closed his eyes. It was peaceful there. Quiet. Finally I realized we had to get going—couldn't stay there forever. Me and Prince slowly stood up.

Wow! Way down yonder, I could see Apache Springs, all of it, at once. It looked like a miniature town that Jesse and me might make in the dirt, with boxes for trailers and tiny toy cars. Only they weren't boxes and toys, they were real. "Look, Prince," I said. "There's our trailer, and there's Ragland's Grocery, and there, that black ribbon, that's the highway through town." This was like when I rode the old Prince high in the air. Only this was better. This was real. And I was thinking, Maybe I don't have to slide down Satan's slide now. Maybe this was good enough. Maybe I ought not to press my luck.

I looked around to see if Prince was admiring the view too. He wasn't. He was sniffing some rocks. Then I discovered I could see the very top of Little Toad now 'cause I was at the top.

Not too far away was what looked to be a pile of rocks. About halfway up was a cave. It didn't look like much, just a hole in the rock pile. All of a sudden—hey, now!—a kitty cat came out of the cave. It didn't see us at first. Then it did. It stopped, dead still. Me and Prince were dead still too. All three. I was wondering what a kitty cat was doing way up here. This cat was taller than Pop's tabby and skinny, real skinny, more skinny than me, and its fur was dull and shabby. It was yellow with brown spots. It had tufts of hair springing out of two pointy ears and a bobbed tail. A bobbed tail? Hold on—that there wudn't no kitty cat. That there was a bobcat!

My heart started up—*da-dum, da-dum.* "Go feet, *go!*" I yelled to my feet. Only feet didn't go. They were froze tight. Bobcat's feet were frozen, too, I saw. We were all froze, staring at each other. Ugly pictures started filling my head. In case you don't know, bobcats are wild animals with dagger claws, sharp as razors, that can tatter hide. As I stared at Mr. Bobcat, I imagined him slinking toward me. Slow at first. Then faster. Soon he'd be running in long graceful strides. When he'd get five feet away, he'd push off with his powerful limbs. I saw him floating in the air, paws out, claws extended. Those dagger claws sharp as razors. He'd hiss at me, baring fangs. It'd be over in no time. I'd lay there—a bloody heap. Mr. Bobcat'd strip the flesh off my bones till no more Dodi. Just my skeleton bleaching in the sun and scraps of clothing fluttering in the breeze. When I didn't show for dinner, Momma and Dad'd get worried and come looking for me. They'd get Pop and Mrs. Robinson to help search, Mr. Ragland too. They'd stumble across my bones, but they wouldn't be able to tell it was me. I'd try to yell out, "*Stop. Wait.* It's me. It's your Dodi. Don't you recognize me?"

But I couldn't yell it out. I couldn't yell. And I couldn't move. I was what they call paralyzed with fear. Sometimes being blessed with an active imagination is not a good thing.

The bobcat twitched his tail, twisted his ears around. I didn't reckon he was saying howdy. I was about to become Mr. Bobcat's dinner, and I couldn't move a muscle. *Ooooo.*

Suddenly Prince went into action. He charged that bobcat. Put his two hind legs in gear and peeled rubber. "Prince," I screamed. "No!" My voice had returned. But it didn't do no good. Prince kept going full tilt. He had one thing on his mind, getting that cat. Like I said before, Prince is too brave for his own good.

Prince raced to the base of the rock pile and jumped high as he could. He landed on one of the rocks, lost his balance, and came tumbling down. Got up and tried again. Then again. But he couldn't get a foothold. He ran back and forth, looking for a way up. There wudn't one. Finally he put his front paws up high as he could, then barked and snarled and growled and foamed at the mouth. He put on a good show. But that bobcat was long gone. As soon as he saw Prince tear after him, he turned, and as easy as you please, he scampered up and over the rocks and out of sight. He sure didn't care to tangle with a half-crazed dog.

When I figgered that bobcat had had enough time to get to the next county, I went over to Prince, took ahold of him, and pulled him away. He didn't want to leave. He kept trying to break free of my grip.

I'd pulled him across Little Toad and halfway across Big and was wondering if I was going to have to wrangle him all the way back to Apache Springs when suddenly my legs flew out, setting me down hard. Next thing I knew I was sliding down Big Toad. I reached out my hands to slow when I noticed loose gravel racing me down the mountain. I was in a channel worn away by lots of seaters like mine. I was in Satan's slide! That Prince—I was so busy wrestling him along I took no mind of where I was. I considered dragging my hands in the rocks to stop my slide, but—ouch—only for a second. No, I figgered, don't fight it. So I tucked in my elbows, tucked up my knees, tucked down my chin, and away I went. When I got to the drop-off, over I shot, landing on my behind, and away I went again. *Yee-hah!* I was moving. The wind was lifting my hair. The mountain was flying by.

When I got near the bottom, the slide flattened,

and I slowed down. I saw a black flash out of the corner of my eye. It was Prince, pedaling four little legs as fast as he could. He was racing me to the bottom, that rascal. I'd plumb forgot about him, my mind being on lasting through the slide with my hide intact. Up at the top, while I was flying, I was saying a little prayer so's I didn't come off the mountain in pieces. Now that I had slowed some, I wanted to speed up to beat Prince, and I paddled the ground with my heels.

Prince beat me to the bottom. In fact, he reached bottom, raced back to pounce on my chest, then raced back down again to beat me a second time. Show-off. But that was fine by me.

"Prince," I said, "you saved my life. You scared off Mr. Bobcat. If he'd caught me here by myself, I would have been on the losing end of fangs and claws." So that was that. Prince was my bestest friend now. It was him for me. And me for him. Forever and ever, and always.

I took his head in my hands. "Prince, please, please, please be good. You rascal, you." I placed a kiss on his nose. "I love you, Prince." He gave me a slobbery lick in return.

✿ ✿ ✿

On the way home, I stopped by Mrs. Robinson's to say I was real sorry for the mess Prince'd made. If you want to know the truth, I thought about not saying anything, then pleading ignorance when asked about it. But Momma would have seen through that, and then I'd have gotten into even deeper Dutch. I've learned, the hard way, that it's better to fess up and take your punishment.

But, guess what? Mrs. Robinson hadn't told Momma on us. I don't think she was going to. See, I told you she was nice. She said she could transplant a batch of the bubble-gum flowers into the bare patch, and in a few weeks you wouldn't be able to tell that ugly brown spot had ever been there. Said me and Prince could help. We went over the next morning to do so. Prince watched, not looking a bit sorry for all the trouble he had caused. Then later I helped pull weeds. I had the dickens telling what was flower and what was weed no matter how often Mrs. Robinson told me.

CHAPTER

13

I begged Prince, please, please be good. But I guess he wudn't listening. A couple of weeks later, something real exciting happened. As usual, Prince was smack-dab in the middle of it.

It was Sunday. On Sundays, Momma cooks one big early meal in place of the two littler lunch and supper. This Sunday, Momma had cooked pot roast with glazed carrots and russet potatoes. There was a green salad with cherry tomatoes, some canned biscuits, and for dessert, chocolate cream pie from Ragland's. Yum. I should say me and Momma made the supper, because I was in the kitchen the good part of the morning, scraping carrots and cutting up salad fixings.

Everyone was crowded around the table: me, Mickey and Mac, Momma, Daddy, then Jesse. The twins sat between me and Momma so we could cut their food into teensy pieces and try to get them to mind their manners. Ha, trying to get them to mind their manners was like trying to teach a hog to nibble its slop at chow time. Mac was two inches taller than Mickey on account of his high chair being bigger. No one had room to move much, being as how there was so many of us and so little table. I sat closest to the kitchen counter. It was my job to stand up, reach over and take hold of each dish, and pass it around. Some were heavy, and I had to be careful not to pitch one on the floor. Never have though.

Prince was tied outside to the front steps like he was suppose to be. The slats on the door were open, and every now and then I heard him whine. I reckoned the pot roast was firing up his juices. I figgered to sneak him some scraps when everyone had cleared out, and I was cleaning up.

Daddy said, "Roast, Dodi."

I stood up and reached behind me for the platter. Momma held it while Daddy slid off a piece then passed it back to me. I stood up and put it back on the counter.

Then Jesse said, "Roast." So I had to stand up again and reach around for the platter and pass it over to him. He left me holding it while he took his merry time picking out a piece.

"Hurry up, will you?" I said. My arms were about to break. "You're slower than frozen snot." That brought a *swat* on my arm from Momma. "Well, make him hurry up then," I said, "before my arm falls off."

He took off a hunk. I straightened up and put the platter back on the counter and glared at him. And he gave me a smirk in return. So I stuck out my tongue. He scooched down to kick me under the table, but I saw it coming and swung my leg out of the way, and he kicked the chair leg instead.

Then *swat* again.

"What's that for?" I asked, rubbing the top of my arm, which was getting dadblamed sore.

"Your daddy wants more potatoes. Maybe if you tended to your own business, you'd hear," said

Momma. Daddy wasn't saying much. He must have been worrying about something. I hoped he wudn't worrying about my dog, and all the trouble he was getting into and maybe could get into in the future, given half a chance. So I decided to be on my extra-special behavior and not carry on any while he was trying to eat.

But that Jesse was smirking at me again. I crossed my eyes at him and called him a ninny. Only I didn't say the word out loud. I only mouthed it so nothing came out. He don't like being called a ninny, even if he is one and even if it ain't said out loud, so he scooched down in his chair to kick me under the table again. He missed and hit my chair leg a second time.

The twins were jabbering between themselves and making a mess in their food and eating like this was the only meal they'd had all day. It wudn't.

Then Jesse, who has to get the last word in, said, "Mom, Dodi called me a name."

"No, I didn't," I said. I did, but I didn't 'cause like I said, nothing came out.

"You two be quiet," said Momma. "I don't want to hear another peep out of either one of you." She said, looking at me, "We are going to eat the rest of our meal in peace and quiet." Then she rubbed her forehead like she had a headache coming on. Everything got quiet except the swamp cooler and the clink of flatware hitting plates.

Then Prince started barking. I decided to pay it no mind, figgering it was just Pop's tabby walking by and Prince would stop soon as she passed. But he didn't stop. He kept barking and barking. Sometimes he would stop to draw breath, then start up again. I began to squirm in my seat because you know who was about to get it again. But this was when Daddy looked up and out the window. He stared, and his eyes got big. No one could tell what he was staring at as we were crammed so tight, we couldn't wiggle around to see.

Then—whoa!—Daddy was out of his chair and out the door. He was gone so fast, he was just a blur. The rest of us sat there with our mouths open, wondering, What in tarnation?

Then we got up and rushed to the door. Jesse made it first, then me, then Momma. The twins were left strapped in their high chairs. I heard them start to kick up a fuss as I went tearing down the steps. Prince was barking and running back and forth, his chain pulled tight. He lunged at me but missed. He almost tripped me up, but I was moving. I was all the way to the end of the yard when I heard the door slam open against the side of our trailer. I ignored it. I had something else on my mind.

It was the Bulldog's trailer. It was on fire. There were puffs of ugly smoke coming out, more smoke than I ever saw, pouring out the doors and window cracks. If I'd taken the time to look, I'd have noticed that my dad wudn't around, but I didn't. I don't reckon any of us did. We were standing there, gawking at that on-fire trailer, watching the smoke getting thicker and blacker.

Next thing, the front door to the trailer burst open. Out came Daddy. He came tumbling down the steps in a roll of smoke, rubbing his eyes and coughing. Why, that was where my dad was. As soon as he saw that fire, he'd charged in. He didn't stop to think on it because he knew the Bulldog, Mizz Bullock, could be asleep in there. Nobody, not even that meanie, deserved to be bar-be-qued.

He went over to Momma. I heard him say, "Nobody home." Then he went on past us. He picked up our water hose. He turned the spigot and started to squirt the burning trailer. I looked around. There was a crowd of people. I'll bet everyone from the park was there, except the Bulldog. Two men had hoses and were doing the same thing as my dad: squirting the burning trailer. But I could tell, that trailer was a goner.

The flames were shooting out of it. I felt like I had my face up against our electric heater. Now and again a breeze would come out of nowhere and fan my face and make me shiver. But I didn't pay it no mind. I just stood there, staring like the other folks. Then the men directed their hoses to the little add-on room at the back end of the trailer. I reckon they thought they might be able to save it. They soaked it down good.

Then my dad turned around and trotted over to our trailer and started squirting it, and the yard too. Right away, the other two men with hoses did the same thing. Those flames got close, but they didn't catch our trailer. The other trailers in the park were spread out enough so's not to be in danger. Before you knew it, the fire had burned itself out. It all happened so fast, I didn't have time to think about us losing our trailer and all our toys burning up and having no place to sleep except the hard old dirt. And I didn't have time to think about what if the Bulldog *had* been inside her trailer and what if she'd gotten burned up too. And then me and Prince would have spent the rest of our days feeling guilty that we hadn't been nicer to her. I guess it was a good thing I didn't have time to think about all that.

After a while, the people started to leave. The excitement was over. All's that was left of the Bulldog's trailer was the skin, scarred and flimsy like charred tinfoil. But the add-on was still there. Its window had shattered and it was scorched, but it had been saved from the fire. Inside it I could see lots of snapshots of old people and little doodads. Didn't look like much to me. I'd always wondered what she had in there.

Me and Momma and Daddy and Jesse were still staring at the burned-out mess when I heard a noise behind me. I turned. It was the Bulldog. She must have been at the Desert Rose, cooling off from the heat with a cold beer. I guess someone went over there and told her the bad news. She'd run all the way back; she was wheezing and clutching her stomach.

She stopped when she got to the edge of the patio. She stood there and stared. Her face was pasty white like glue. Her eyes were watery. I don't think it was from the smoke; it was purd near gone. Hers was just an old trailer long since faded from the sun with a tiny add-on, but I guess it was all she had. Now she just had her add-on. And her patio, of course. Cement patios don't burn—good thing. Momma went over and put her arm around Mizz Bullock and started talking to her.

Daddy nudged me. "Come on, let's go on back. Nothing more we can do here." I started toward our trailer.

I reached the door and climbed the steps. When I peered in, I saw the twins in their high chairs, faces streaked. Mac, his head on his tray, had gone to sleep. Mickey was rubbing brown and yellow goop in his hair with two pudgy hands. Their food was everywhere: streaking their shirts, dribbling off the high chairs, and plopped on the linoleum.

And there, smack-dab in the middle of the table,

was Prince. He took no notice of me. He had eaten the food off all our plates and was now devouring the store-bought chocolate cream pie. His chain trailed behind him, out the front door to the steps, where it was still attached. Oh dear, oh dear. I didn't get a chance to yell "Scat!" before Jesse and Daddy came up and crowded in behind. A powerful fear gripped me. Oh, Prince, what have you done? You're as good as gone now. Ain't nothing I can say nor do will save your sorry hide this time. All was quiet.

Suddenly I heard this roarlike noise behind me. I turned around. It was Daddy. He was laughing, big donkey hee-haws. He let loose like he had been saving up that laugh for a long time, and it was a pure relief to let it out. Me and Jesse stared at him. He was holding his sides. His eyes were watering, like what happens when you laugh too hard. I wondered if all that smoke had caused him to take leave of his senses? I turned again to Prince. His head was deep in pie, his tongue was going to town, and his tail was a-wagging. His stomach looked round and swollen as a ripe tomato. All of a sudden, he looked up at us. He had a chocolate cream beard, chocolate cream

eyebrows, with a dollop of whipped cream topping his nose. I had to admit, he did look comical. I couldn't help myself; I started laughing. Jesse too. So there we were, staring in at our ruined dinner, laughing to bust a gut. Don't that beat all?

After a while, I heard this sigh from Daddy. He glanced back at Momma, who was still with Mizz Bullock. He said, "Well, looks like Prince got his Sunday dinner too. Now why don't you, little missy"—he tapped me on the shoulder—"take him on outside. Then come in and clean up this mess for your mom."

"Yessirree," I said loud, in relief. I went and tugged on Prince's chain. He hopped down to Daddy's chair and then to the floor, and followed me out the door, Mr. Meek, now the damage was done. Then I came in and cleaned up the mess. Daddy made Jesse help. That set him to grumbling. And you know what? Daddy didn't say another word about Prince messing up.

CHAPTER

14

This should be the end of my story. Since no more mention was made of the Sunday dinner disaster, I thought sure 'nuff Momma and Daddy had decided Prince could stay. Plus having the Bulldog out of my life, the future was looking as rosy as a desert sunset. One bad thing, though, school had started.

That was where I was, walking home from the first day of Miss Bigger's third grade. I was banging my lunch box in time with a tune playing in my head when I pulled up short. There in the Bulldog's spot was a strange trailer. It was on the dumpy side, streaked with rust and showing a couple of dents— no improvement from what had been there. Except in one way—it was new, meaning this here was a new family, meaning maybe they had a little girl.

I stood there eyeballing that trailer, willing there to be a girl my age inside. Even close to my age would be okay; she wouldn't have to be exactly my age. Not even the same grade. Just close. The more I stared, the more convinced I became that there really was a girl sitting behind that trailer door, cooling off under the swamp cooler. After all, things were starting to go my way, or so I thought.

There was only one way to find out. I took off across the patio. Before I got to the trailer, *swoosh*, the door flew open. It came whistling by me like a runaway train. Liked to have knocked my block off. And who should come clumping down the stairs—the Bulldog. I stood there staring, mouth open.

She spied me out of the corner of her eye, whirled around, and spit out, "Well, what do you want?"

Let me tell you, when you've convinced yourself a little girl is going to come bouncing down those steps and out stomps a jowl-faced Bulldog, it's like having the stuffing knocked out of you. So it took a few seconds before I could stammer out, "Nothing."

"Nothing," she said. "Then what are you doing here? In *my* yard?" She narrowed her eyes at me, "Don't tell me I'm still going to have trouble with you."

"No ma'am, I . . . ," I started to say. I turned to skedaddle. I got to the edge of her yard when I heard her say, "Dodi. Hold up." Uh-oh. I stopped dead in my tracks. I turned slow, ready to run.

She cleared her throat. Took her a long time to get the words out. Then the Bulldog tells me that my dad had mentioned that Prince's barking had alerted everyone to the fire and that allowed them to save her add-on. Only she didn't say Prince. She said "that mutt." "Might have saved me too," she mumbled, "if I'd been inside, taking my siesta like most afternoons. . . . Course, I wasn't," she added.

By now, of course, I had realized that the Bulldog had gotten herself another trailer and had it parked where the old one had been. You'd of thought she'd of had it towed clean on t'other side of the park, just to get away from yours truly. But maybe she was lonely. I guess even Bulldogs need company. Then I was struck with a thought: A dog is what she needs. A cute little dog like Prince. After all, he cured my loneliness. Why, that would be great. Then Prince could have him a playmate for when I'm at school.

"Whyn't you get you a dog?" I said.

"What?"

"Then you wouldn't have to depend on Prince's barking when your trailer's on fire, 'cause your own dog would sniff it out and bark. And your dog could keep you company, like Prince does me. And he— or she, 'cause maybe you'll get a girl dog—could keep Prince company when I'm at school. They could play together." I looked up, grinning. I'd hit on one dandy idea.

She narrowed her eyes at me. "You've got to be kidding. What do I need with another dog to clean up after? One is all I'm fixing to put up with. *Sheesh*," she added, shaking her head back and forth. The Bulldog then turned to go inside her trailer. I heard her mumble, "Just what I need . . . mumble, mumble . . . hole in the head . . . mumble, mumble . . . nonsense," just before the door slammed shut.

I guess she didn't think it was such a dandy idea. Oh, well. I started toward home. There was Prince, straining his chain, wagging his tail at me, wiggling back and forth. I kneeled down to pet him. He jumped and ka-chunked me under the chin.

"How you doing, boy? You miss me?" He must have, because he reared up and knocked me on my behind and started slobbering me with doggie kisses.

"See that trailer back there?" I said to him, and pointed. "That's the Bulldog's. She's back. So's you and me still got to watch it. After all, she doesn't need another dog to clean up after. One . . ."

Wait a dadgum minute. What did she mean by that—one dog was all she was going to put up with? Heck, there was only *one* dog—Prince. Hmm.

Well, I'll be.

I took Prince's face between my hands and peered into those black marbly eyes. "Yup," I said. "Just like I told you. It's you and me, Prince. Bestest friends. Forever and ever, and always. Yessirree."

You rascal, you.